CHRISTMAS WITH THE SANTA BEARS™

Written by Thomas McInerney • Illustrated by Pattie Silver-Thompson

MODERN PUBLISHING

A Division of Unisystems, Inc.
New York, New York 10022
Printed in Singapore

D1307882

It was Christmas Eve in Santa's workshop, and every room was filled with toys. There were basketballs and soccer balls and crystal balls and bells. There were wagons and catcher's mitts and crayons and wooden soldiers. There were dolls in lace dresses, all wearing pink hats, and great

piles of smiling teddy bears chatting in the corner. Cuddly cotton kittens and furry, wind-up puppies were playing on the floor.

Santa's elves were frantically boxing and bagging, and even Mrs. Santa was lending a hand with the bows.

Everyone was so busy inside the workshop, that no one looked outside. There was a blizzard raging! There was so much snow, Santa's reindeer could barely see in through the workshop's windows.

Suddenly, Mrs. Santa noticed. "Oh no!" she cried. "Look outside!" Santa and all the elves looked up from their work. "If this storm keeps up, we'll be snowed in," she said. "What will we do?" she asked Santa.

One by one, the elves looked out the window. "We already are snowed in!" they whispered to each other.

"Summon the chief elf!" shouted Santa. "And tell him to bring the Elf Horn!" he added.

In moments, the chief elf was tugging at Santa's coat. "Will we have to call the Santa Bears?" he asked anxiously. It had been many years since Santa had relied upon the Elf Horn's magic and called the legendary Santa Bears for help.

"Yes," replied Santa with no doubt whatsoever. He knew in his heart that if the Santa Bears didn't help him there'd be no Christmas.

All the elf elders shook their heads knowingly, while the youngest elves clapped their hands and whispered with glee, "At last, at last. We're calling the Santa Bears! Yippee!"

Then, proudly, the chief elf scrambled up the chimney and blew into the golden trumpet.

While Santa and Mrs. Santa and the elves and the reindeer listened, the elf tune worked its way out of the horn little by little. At first it was a soft sound. But soon it became louder and louder until it sounded like thunder. Its melody went from every mountain to every valley, to . . .

. . . a small cozy cabin at the farthest end of the North Pole where Mama Polar Bear and her cubs were celebrating Christmas Eve. As they added the last touches to their sparkling Christmas tree the cubs began to shout, "Tell us about the Elf Horn and why we're called the Santa Bears, Mama."

But just as Mama was about to begin the legend the

cubs already knew by heart, she heard the marvelous melody of the magical Elf Horn . . . and so did the cubs!

"Santa must need the Santa Bears!" the excited cubs shouted in unison. "Let's go! Let's go!" they whooped as they jumped up and down.

"What a special Christmas it's going to be for my little cubs," Mama Polar Bear sighed as she readied them for their first adventure as full-fledged Santa Bears!

"Come on," Mama called to the cubs as she led them through the storm over the deep snow drifts and icy patches.

The cubs hurried along. They knew if they didn't arrive in time to help Santa there'd be no Christmas . . . and no presents . . . and no Christmas carols . . . and no candy canes. Suddenly, they ran as fast as they could!

They traveled for a long, long time, skidding and sliding and sloshing about.

"The ice sure is slippery!" said the littlest cub as he inched his way along. Then his feet flip-flopped and he fell toward a hole in the ice. There was a great big splash and the littlest cub was bobbed up into the air atop the tip of a playful seal's nose!

"Whoopee," he yelled as he landed 'kerplunk' in the snow. Then the seal swam away with a smile as the bears trudged onward.

Only such strong bears could make such a journey!

Much later they came to the edge of an iceberg. "How will we ever get across?" asked one of the very tired cubs.

"I have an idea," said Mama Polar Bear as she stretched her toes and reached her arms across the opening from one side to the other—like a bridge.

The cubs gently tiptoed over her and then Mama raised herself higher and higher until she somersaulted to the other side to join the cubs.

Only such courageous bears could make such a trek!

At last Mama Polar Bear and the cubs reached Santa's workshop.

"Santa's snowed in!" hollered the cubs.

"That's why he sounded the magic Elf Horn!" added Mama Polar Bear.

"And that's why he needs the Santa Bears," they roared as only Santa Bears could.

Inside the workshop, Santa and Mrs. Santa and the elves jumped for joy as they watched the Santa Bears spring into action.

Mama Polar Bear summoned all of her strength and began to shovel and scoop the snow away. The little cubs climbed to the top of the workshop and rolled down the snowdrifts like huge snowballs that tumbled down the hill and crumbled at the bottom.

Only such mighty bears could have worked so hard!

"We've been rescued," shouted the elves.
"I knew only the Santa Bears could save Christmas!"
Santa said as he smiled warmly and hugged his bears. "I
never doubted for a moment that you'd get here!"

"But now Christmas is almost here and we must still load up the sled," he added. As they helped Santa pack, the little bears marveled at all the toys.

There were boxes of yo-yos and bushels of banjos. There were bags full of books and big trunks brimming with toy trucks. Everything was piled onto the sleigh until it was filled to overflowing. Then Santa jumped into the driver's seat—his reindeer were ready!

"But wait," shouted Santa as everyone stood there in wonder. "The littlest Santa Bears must come with me to help deliver these presents all around the world."

Mama was proud as her cubs bounded into the sleigh next to Santa. In a moment they were all up, up and away flying high over the North Pole. They could see the whole world by starlight, and every city was twinkling with Christmas spirit.

The Santa Bears hugged each other—and Santa Claus, too. They giggled as the sleigh sped past the smiling full moon.

This was a Christmas they would never forget!